Where did my marks go?

Written by Alex Goh
Illustrated by Tan Liqing Vivien

Where Did My Marks Go?

Written by Alex Goh
Edited by Vivian Yuen
Illustrated by Tan Liqing VIvien

© 2022

ISBN 978-981-18-5778-2 (Paperback)
ISBN 978-981-18-5778-2 (Digital)

where did my marks go

Written by Alex Goh
Illustrated by Tan Liqing Vivien

Clara is a bright and helpful student.
She answers all the questions in class.
She plays well with all her friends.

1

Clara is in kindergarten. Her teacher, Miss Judy, has decided to have a spelling test for the class next week, and she wants the students to memorise a list of words. Clara immediately starts to memorise the words.

Mom and Dad helped Clara prepare for the test from morning to night, and even during dinner and showers!

With Mom and Dad's help, Clara was confident and prepared to ace the test.

4

It was a Tuesday. The day of the test had arrived. Clara was nervous.

Miss Judy said: "Class, please sit away from each other, and no peeking at your friends' answers!"

Clara was handed a piece of paper.
She took out a pencil to write her name.

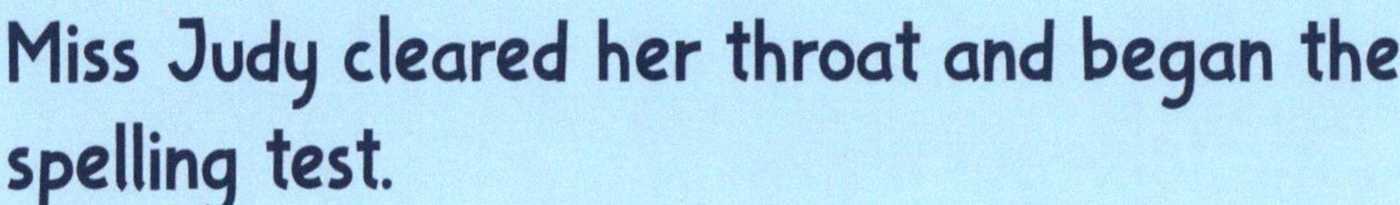

Miss Judy cleared her throat and began the spelling test.

"Apple."

It was an easy first word.

"Banana."

The second word was easy too.

"Proper."

"Probably."

7

Clara's mind went blank. She knew the word but was not able to remember how to spell it. Clara began to become anxious. Mom and Dad had practised with her so many times!

"Pineapple."

Clara did not hear the word and missed it.
She started to *panic*.

Soon, the test was over, and she had received a score of 80/100.

Clara showed her marks to her Mom and Dad. They were upset about her results and scolded her.

"With these marks, how can you become a doctor? You can only be a shopkeeper and a hawker!", Mom exclaimed.

Clara went to bed crying. She cried, and cried, and cried herself to sleep.

Soon, Clara fell asleep and dreamt. In her dream, she was as light as a feather. She could fly!

To her surprise, Clara's test paper had also come to life!

"Hi Clara, my name is Eighties! I am looking for Twenties. Can you come with me on a quest to find it?"

Clara hesitated.

"I'm not sure if I will be of any help."

Eighties replied, "Not to worry, Clara. We can do this together."

Clara and Eighties began their quest flying down a street of shophouses and restaurants.

Soon, Clara and Eighties walked into a flower store and met a florist.

"Hello, Miss. I am looking for Twenties. Have you seen it?"

The florist replied, "Hello! No, I have not seen Twenties, but I found Five. Do you want it?"

"Oh no, I do not think that is the correct number."

"How did you get Five?"

The florist replied, "I scored 5 for a test that I did when I was 10 years old. That is how I found Five."

"What are you doing now?"

"This is my shop! I sell flowers to people."

"My parents said that I will grow up to be unsuccessful. Is that true?"

"That is not true! Look at me – I am happy as I can be. I may not be good at tests, but I am good at talking to people and making them feel comfortable."

"Do not worry, Clara. You have many opportunities to discover what you are good at."

Eighties took Clara by the hand and flew away together to a nearby hawker centre. They were looking for clues to finding Twenties. They came across a store that sold Nasi Lemak.

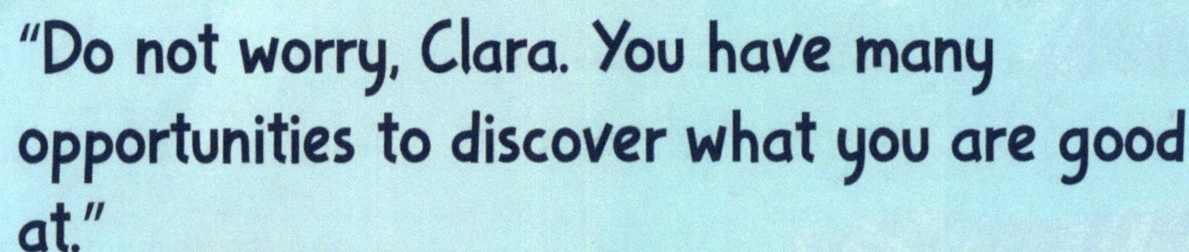

"Hello, Aunty, have you seen Twenties around here? We are finding it."

"Hi Clara, I have not seen Twenties. I found Nineties!"

18

"Wow, Aunty, you have such high marks! Why are you selling food at a hawker centre? You can be a doctor!"

"Yes, I have high marks, but I did not want to be a doctor. I like to cook good food for people. That is why I chose to open a store that sells Nasi Lemak."

"Well, I do not know how to cook. I do not think my food will taste nice."

"Do not worry, Clara. You can always learn to cook. I can teach you my secret Nasi Lemak recipe when you are older!"

20

Clara smiled excitedly.

Then, Eighties took Clara to a clinic to look for clues to finding Twenties.

"Hello, Doctor. Have you seen Twenties? We are on the quest to find it!"

"Hello Doctor, if you scored 50, how did you become a doctor?"

"I worked very hard and had lots of help from people around me."

"Doctor, do you think I can be like you too?"

"Of course, only if you believe it and work towards it."

Eighties took Clara's hand and flew back home.

"Seems like there are no clues for us in finding Twenties. What should we do?"

"Eighties, I know where Twenties is!"

Clara reached into her pocket, and Twenties was there!

"After talking to everyone, I realise that the missing marks we were searching for do not matter. I should not worry about my marks, but continue to learn and discover what I am good at."

Do what
I like
and for
myself
80

Clara woke up from the dream smiling.

She was happy to know that she could be anything she wanted to be if she put her mind to it.

29

Sharing Questions

1. Why did Clara cry?
2. What happened to Clara in the end?
3. What should Clara tell her parents after the dream?
4. Do you think the doctor in the dream is smart?
5. Why did Clara find twenties in her pocket?

Synopsis

Six-year-old Clara is the star pupil at her kindergarten. Witty and friendly, she's often praised for her grades and gets along easily with others. As a star pupil, Clara has high expectations for herself and aims to give her best in all her tests. Her parents tell her that getting high marks is the key to being a successful adult. One day, despite studying all week for a spelling test, she suddenly forgets all that she revised.

Receiving less-than-perfect marks, Clara goes home in tears. At night, she falls into a deep dream, and embarks on a journey of a lifetime full of surprises, fun and flying (yes, flying in the air!) to discover that, perhaps, success is more than high marks on a test paper. "Hello, Clara. No, I have not seen Twenties, but I found Fifty. Is that close enough?"